D0817655

ZOOM BROOM

Margie Palatini
Illustrated by Howard Fine

SCHOLASTIC INC.
New York Toronto London Auckland Sydney
Mexico City New Delhi Hong Kong

No part of this publication may be reproduced in whole or in part, or stored in
a retrieval system, or transmitted in any form or by any means, electronic, mechanical, photo-
copying, recording, or otherwise, without written permission of the publisher.
For information regarding permission, write to Hyperion Books for Children, an imprint
of Buena Vista Books, Inc., 114 Fifth Avenue, New York, NY 10011-5690.

ISBN 0-439-07441-X

Text copyright © 1998 by Margie Palatini.
Illustrations copyright © 1998 by Howard Fine.
All rights reserved. Published by Scholastic Inc.,
555 Broadway, New York, NY 10012,
by arrangement with Hyperion Books for Children,
an imprint of Buena Vista Books, Inc.

SCHOLASTIC and associated logos are trademarks
and/or registered trademarks of Scholastic Inc.

12 11 10 9 8 7 6 5 4 3 2 1   9/9 0 1 2 3 4/0

Printed in the U.S.A.   08

First Scholastic printing, October 1999

This book is set in 15-point Publius.
Designed by Stephanie Bart-Horvath.

For Jamie—still my best one and only
—M. P.

For my son Benjamin,
for all the joy he brings me—H. F.

Gritch the Witch plunked down in her batwing chair with a dusty KER-PLOP.

She propped up her tootsies, uncurled her toes, then warmed those thirteen delicate digits by the roaring fire.

Gritch dunked a *batscotti* into a bubbling brew of *eek!spresso* and crunched down on the cookie with her good front tooth.

She slurped. She slobbered. She smacked her lips.

Those crispy winged cookies were *so* tasty.

But as tasty as they were—and they were tasty, make no mistake about that—Gritch's belly still grumbled for something more.

A nibble that was just a *bit* more filling. Fattening. Furry.

Gritch grinned. "Yes! Yes! Rabbit Rye!" she cackled with a drool.

She always did have a hankering for a hunk of hare.

"Mmm-mmm-mmm. Nothing better than the aroma of hot baking Bunny Bread," Gritch said with a snort.

She gave her fingers a snap. She knew just where to find those jumping jackrabbits, too. **No problem!** The Farmer in the Dell had a bunch of bunnies hopping all over his place.

So with a Hi-ho and a Der-io, Gritch grabbed her hat, to her broom gave a whistle, and away they all flew like . . .

And away they all flew like . . .

"Huh? There's a teeny little PROBLEM!" Gritch shrieked as she stalled in midair.

The old broom just couldn't get it in gear. The stick was stuck!

It spit. Sputtered. Coughed. Chugged. Choked. And then it gave out a long gasping, gurgly gurgle, did one loop-d-loop, and tailspinned toward ground zero.

"What the WHOAAAAAA! How the OOOOOOWWWW! What the HEY! HEY! HEY!"

K-BOOM!

"Hay!" she spat.

Gritch moaned. She groaned. She oohed and oiched. And then wobbled and hobbled over to what was left of her old broomstick. It was not a pretty sight.

"I've seen toothpicks better-looking than this!" she squawked, still spitting splinters and kicking straw.

"Now what am I going to do?" she wailed. "How can I get to where I want to go—when I can't go to where I want to get—to get what I want!"

Forget snaring hares and baking a batch of Bunny Bread. Those toasted tails would have to wait. This witch needed a broom. A broom that zipped. Zapped. Zoomed!

Now how could she get one of those, she wondered, as she tapped her lucky wart.

"Who can I turn to?" Gritch said as she fingered through her address book.

"There's the Witch of the West. Maybe I can borrow a broom from her? No. Poor dear had a meltdown . . .

"Hmmm. The Witch of the East? No. Old gal had one of those awful 'house' accidents . . .

"Let's see. Let's see," Gritch muttered. "Aha! Yes! Yes! The Witch in the Woods! She never leaves that sweet little cottage. I'll just borrow a broom from her!" Gritch declared, already limping down the lane. "That shouldn't be a problem . . . PROBLEM!"

Uh-oh. She screeched to a halt.

"Drats!" Gritch grumbled. "I can't go over there. She has those kids, Hansel and Gretel, living with her . . . Eeesh! There's something about those two I just don't trust. They look at me . . . the way I look at them. Yikes!"

Gritch decided it was best not to borrow a broom. She would just buy one.

So she hoofed it on over to Foxy's for the best deal in town.

"Well, howdy-do and welcome to you," said the salesman. He rushed over to Gritch before her big toe could hit the showroom floor.

"Allow me, Madam. My card. My card."

He took Gritch by the arm. "Looking for some new transportation, are you? Well, you've come to the right place! I can see you're a lady of quality. Distinction. Definite taste!"

"Hold your sloppy choppers right there, bud," said Gritch as Foxy rolled back his tongue. "I want a—"

"Don't say another word," interrupted the fox. "I know just what you're looking for. Tell you what I'm going to do," he said with a clap. "Going to roll out the red carpet for you.

"Yessiree. Lookee here. Straight from A Lad in the East. It's plush. It's lush. Tassle-free! You'll feel like you're floating on air!"

"A rug?" Gritch groused with a glare.

"I don't want a rug!"

"Okey-dokey, little lady. Okey-dokey. You say no rug, then no rug. Tell you what I'm going to do," he said with a clap. "Special for you. Just until midnight. This magical little number right here. Fit for a princess. Very low mileage. Used only once. Runs like a charm. What's that you say? Don't like the color orange? For you—we can paint it! We can paint it!"

"A PUMPKIN?" Gritch grumbled with a stare. "I don't want a pumpkin!"

"Absolutely, little lady! Absolutely! You say no pumpkin, then no pumpkin! The vegetable look doesn't appeal to you. Fine. Dandy. Tell you what I'm going to do," the fox said with a clap. "Maybe a . . ."

"Save the spiel, cut the chit-chat, and can the flim-flam, Foxy!" shouted Gritch into the salesman's snout. "My legs are pooped and my tootsies are toasted. Ditch the pitch. I want a broom! A Zoom Broom. A stick that's quick. A power launch. Get it?"

"Got it."

"Good."

"Right this way, little lady," said the fox. "Right this way. A Zoom Broom you want. A Zoom Broom you'll get. Why didn't you say so? Yessiree. The best brooms you can buy. Pick any you want."

"Oh, my!" exclaimed Gritch, seeing all the brooms. "There are so many to choose from! This one? Or that one? I don't know. Which one is the one I want?"

"Okey-dokey, little lady!" Foxy said with a clap. "WITCH 1 is the one you want."

"That's what I just said, you flaky fox! *Which one* is the one I want?"

"Fine with me," said he. "WITCH 1."

"That's what I'm asking you! *Which one* is the Zoom Broom?"

"WITCH 1 is a Zoom Broom. That's right," said the fox.

"What's right?" said Gritch.

"It's right. Right on the left."

"Left? I don't want any old brooms that are left, you flim-flamming fleecer! I want a new one. A Zoom Broom! You fox-trotting floor flusher! Give me *ONE*."

The fox gulped. "Anything you say, madam. Then I'll wrap up WITCH 1."

"*Which one?* ANY ONE!" screeched Gritch.
"*That one*," she pointed.

"Oooh! You want *that broom*," sighed the fox. "So you want 2!"

"TWO?" wailed the witch. "I don't want two. What would I do with *two* brooms? I want one broom. ONE! ONE! ONE!"

The fox uncurled his nose. He took a deep breath and gritted his teeth.

"Fine, little lady," he said unruffling his fur. "Then it's Witch 1."

"That's what I'm asking you!" groaned Gritch. "Which one? You're giving me such a PROBLEM!"

The fox sighed. "Perhaps, little lady, you should forget about the broom."

"Forget about the broom? HELL-OOOO!" she screeched. "I need a broom, you ninny. I'm a witch, remember?"

"Oh, so, you're a witch," said the fox, losing his patience. "So what?"

Gritch glared. She stared. She screeched, squealed, squawked, kicked, stomped.

"SO WHAT? SO WHAT? SO WHAT?" Gritch stopped stomping. "Wait a minute. You're right. So what?"

After all, she thought, even a broom with zip, zap, and zoom was probably just *too* old-fashioned for a witch with her style. Why, with her brains, beauty, and talent she could make anything fly!

"Okay there, Foxy. Give me something hip. Something hot. Something happening!"

"A classic," said the fox. "It's
you! Care to take it for a spin?"
the fox said,
dangling the key.

"Spin?" Gritch gave a hoot.

"Under my spell, this baby is
Greased Lightning!"

"Top down?" asked the fox.

"The only way to fly," cackled
Gritch, jumping in.

"I must warn you,
little lady," said the fox.
"It gets a bit chilly out
there with the top down . . .
and I see you don't have a *coat*."

Gritch looked at him and grinned.

"Oooooohhhhh. Don't worry about me. I'll think of something, Foxy! **NO PROBLEM!** No problem at all!"

Z-Z-Z-ZZZOOOOOOM!